CHIP'S DAD

Ruth Symes
Illustrated by Tony Kenyon

Rigby

Chip raced down the track. Sweat dripped from his hair into his eyes. He had to win! Chip was wearing his lucky sneakers and he always won when he wore them.

He cleared the last hurdle and came in first. He felt great! This was only practice— he would do even better on the day of the race!

Eddie slapped him on the back.

"Good race!" he panted.

"Yeah, it was OK," said Chip, pleased.

"Hey, look, your dad's here," said Eddie with a grin.

Chip's heart sank. Turning his head he
saw the purple van, covered with big
painted flowers. What was Dad *doing,* picking
him up from practice? Chip had *told* him not
to come.

Chip's dad got out of the van and waved cheerfully. Chip pretended he hadn't seen him, but his dad was hard to miss. He was wearing a red baseball cap with two moose horns, one on each side of his head. It was Dad's idea of a joke.

"Great hat!" shouted Eddie, grinning.

"Hi, Dad," said Chip in a flat voice. His dad was *so* embarrassing!

"See you tomorrow, Eddie," mumbled Chip as he walked off with Dad. He hung his head and stared at the ground.

"Why are you here, Dad?" asked Chip. "I told you not to meet me."

"Oh, I don't mind!" said Dad.

Chip sat low in his seat, so no one would spot him in Dad's purple flowered van. His mind was whirring, thinking about how often Dad embarrassed him.

There was the time they went swimming.

"I'll show you how to dive, Chip!"
Dad said.

He climbed to the top of the diving board. Then he remembered he was afraid of heights.

"Go on!" said a girl who was standing in line behind him.

"Jump!" someone else shouted.

But Chip's dad couldn't move. He was frozen with fear. Chip had to find a lifeguard to help his dad down. Lots of people from Chip's school saw what happened.

"How could you *do* this to me?" Chip asked. He was *so* embarrassed.

9

But the very worst time was when Dad took Chip to stay with Justin, Chip's oldest friend. They drove for hours and hours to get there, and Chip was very excited. They arrived late at night, and Chip's dad knocked loudly on the door.

"Yoo-hoo!" Chip's dad shouted up at the window. "Let us in!"

Justin's dad seemed to take forever to get to the door, and when he opened it, Chip understood why. He was standing, bleary-eyed in his pajamas, scratching his head.

"What are you doing here?" Justin's dad asked. "It's the middle of the night. We weren't expecting Chip until next weekend."

That's when Chip realized his dad had the wrong day. Justin's dad looked very tired, and Justin was standing behind him, giggling.

"How could you do this to me?" Chip asked. He was so embarrassed.

"I can't stand it," Chip would moan to Mom. "He's so embarrassing!"

"He's doing his best, and he loves you," was all that Mom would say. "One day you'll understand that."

Dad started the engine, and Chip stopped daydreaming.

"Eddie tells me your big race is coming up soon," said Dad. "Let me know what day, OK? I can't miss that!"

"Leave it to Eddie!" thought Chip. "I bet he's just trying to embarrass me in front of the whole school."

Chip had a letter about the race in his bag. Should he just "forget" to show it to his dad? His dad would never find out, and then Chip wouldn't be embarrassed in front of his friends.

When Chip got home, he tore the letter up and put it in the trash can.

Over the next few days, Chip trained hard. Every morning he jogged to school. His dad kept asking him about the race.

"You will tell me when the school race is, won't you, Chip?" he would ask.

"I promise," Chip would say, with his fingers crossed tightly behind his back.

The day of the race arrived at last.

"I wish my dad was here," Eddie said.
"Where's *your* dad, Chip? I bet he's coming.
Your dad's great."

Chip looked at Eddie in surprise, but Eddie
didn't seem to be joking. Chip suddenly felt
bad about not telling his dad about the race.
He knew his dad really wanted to come, and
Chip had promised to tell him when it was.

The race was a competition between the different classes at school. Chip's team was doing well, but so was Eddie's. The race was going to be close.

It was almost time for Chip's event. Chip opened his sports bag to take out his lucky sneakers. They weren't in his bag!

Chip pulled out everything in the bag— no sneakers. A sick feeling started in his stomach. Where were they?

He suddenly realized he had forgotten his lucky sneakers! How could he have been so careless?

"What's wrong, Chip?" asked Eddie.

"I forgot my lucky sneakers!" said Chip.

"You can run in the sneakers you've got on, can't you?" asked Eddie.

Chip shook his head. Eddie didn't understand. Yes, he could *run* in the sneakers he was wearing —but he couldn't *win* in them. He'd lose, and his class would lose, and it would all be his fault.

"Chip!"

Chip looked around. Dad was running toward him. He was waving Chip's lucky sneakers above his head! They knocked his moose hat off, but Dad didn't stop to pick it up. Chip had never been so glad to see anyone in his life.

"Your lucky sneakers!" Dad gasped.

"Dad!" said Chip. He couldn't believe it! How had Dad known? "Thanks, Dad! You're a lifesaver!"

Chip wanted to say more, to say he was sorry, but there wasn't time.

Chip got to the starting line just before the starter gun fired. He raced down the track and flew over the first hurdle. Chip ran faster than he had ever run before. He shot past people until he was almost in the lead. From the crowd, he heard his dad's voice bellowing, "Come on, Chip! You can do it!"

Lunging forward, Chip shot past Eddie a split second before crossing the finish line. He won!

The crowd went wild! Dad jumped up and down, waving his moose hat in the air.

Chip ran over to him.

"Well done, son!" said Dad. "That was fantastic!"

"But, Dad," said Chip, "how did you know the race was today?"

"I bumped into Eddie's dad," said Dad. "I can't believe you forgot to tell me! I almost missed it."

"I'm really glad you didn't miss it," said Chip, and he meant it.

Chip's class won the race. They were each
given a medal.

"Way to go, Chip!" said Eddie. "You really
deserved to win that!"

Chip looked over at his dad. "No, Eddie,
I don't deserve it," he said, "but I know
who does."

Chip walked over to his dad and put the medal around his dad's neck. Dad grinned and gave Chip a hug. Chip had been wrong. Mom and Eddie were right. It didn't matter what Dad wore, or if he was embarrassing at times.

"Thanks, Dad," said Chip. "I'm really glad you came!"